IRISH CREME KILLER

The INNcredibly Sweet Series, Book 1

SUMMER PRESCOTT

Copyright 2016 Summer Prescott Books

All Rights Reserved. No part of this publication nor any of the information herein may be quoted from, nor reproduced, in any form, including but not limited to: printing, scanning, photocopying, or any other printed, digital, or audio formats, without prior express written consent of the copyright holder.

**This book is a work of fiction. Any similarities to persons, living or dead, places of business, or situations past or present, is completely unintentional.

Chapter 1

Petite blonde Melissa Gladstone-Beckett sat alone in her deserted shop, Cupcakes in Paradise, feeling worn out. She'd baked several dozen cupcakes earlier for an elementary school festival, and had been on her feet all day. Finishing the last dregs of her afternoon coffee, she wearily rose from her chair and turned the sign on the door over to "Closed."

Her latest creation, Luck O' the Irish cupcakes, had been a tremendous hit, and there had already been multiple orders placed for upcoming St. Patty's Day celebrations. She'd used a dark chocolate batter and added sour cream for extra richness. Adding a touch of green food coloring and a dash of crème de menthe into the frosting, she then topped each of the festive cakes with sparkling green sugar and a marzipan shamrock.

Trudging slowly next door to the Beach House B&B, a historic beachside inn in Calgon, Florida, that she owned with her dashing and clever husband, Detective Chas Beckett, the exhausted baker looked forward to a long, hot bath and a quiet dinner for two. Crossing the marble-floored foyer to the locked door that led to the owner's wing of the Inn, Missy punched in the code at the keypad and slipped inside to be greeted enthusiastically by her two best furry friends, Toffee, her aging golden retriever, and Bitsy, her feisty maltipoo.

"I missed you guys, too," she grinned, bending down to scratch between two sets of fluffy ears, while the "girls" tried their best to clean her face of any residual frosting that might be present.

Missy had known that today was going to be especially busy, so she'd made arrangements with Spencer, the handsome young veteran who served as handyman, bartender, and breakfast server at the Inn as well as helping out at the cupcake shop, to give the "girls" their afternoon walk. She felt a bit guilty about not being able to take them, but had made sure their early morning romp on the beach had been a little bit longer than usual. The frolicking canines loved Spencer as much as everyone else, so they'd been as delighted to see him with leashes in hand as they would have been to see their devoted owner.

The pair trotted up the stairs at the heels of their weary human, and settled onto a large, fluffy bathmat in a corner of the enormous master bathroom when Missy started her bath. She sprinkled lavender crystals under the hot running water, and the air was soon scented with the calming essence. Sinking gratefully into the swirling waters, with the jets turned up to massage her aching muscles, she breathed a sigh of relief and leaned her head back, eyes closed.

Missy lost track of time as her aches melted away under the gentle jets, and reluctantly turned them off only when her stomach growled, reminding her that it was nearly dinnertime. She dressed in a pretty but comfortable red knit sundress that clung to her curves in all the right places. She and Chas had both been so busy lately that she wanted to look and feel pretty and give him her undivided adoration and attention tonight.

As if her thoughts had conjured him, her tall, dark, and handsome hubby appeared in the doorway of the master bedroom as Missy sat at her antique vanity, putting up her hair.

"Wow, look at you," he said softly, bending down to kiss her neck. She laughed when the sweet brush of his kiss tickled the sensitive skin below her ear. "I can't wait for all of Calgon to see such a beautiful woman on my arm," Chas grinned appreciatively.

"Well, hopefully all of Calgon won't be at the same restaurant tonight," she teased, carefully fastening tiny glittery silver hoops in her ears.

"No worries, I made a reservation," he replied, sitting down on the turn-of-the-century mahogany bench at the foot of the bed, watching his wife as she finished getting ready.

"You really are lovely," he commented, his gaze warm.

"Thank you, sweetie. I worked at it tonight," she smiled with a faint sigh.

"Everything okay?"

"Yes, just a lot on my mind," Missy shrugged, meeting his eyes in the mirror.

"Can I help?" Chas tried to keep his voice neutral, but was concerned. His wife was a consistently positive person, and hearing her wistful tone had him a bit worried.

"We'll talk about it at dinner," she turned to face him after spritzing on his favorite perfume.

"Mmmm… okay," he moved to her, offering his hand and taking a deep, appreciative whiff. "Ready?"

"Definitely," she nodded, but he noted that her smile seemed a bit forced.

Chas Beckett had no idea what his wife needed to talk to him about, but he could tell by her expression that, whatever it was, it was affecting her profoundly. The table that he'd reserved at their favorite casually upscale seafood restaurant was in a quiet corner overlooking the water, so they'd have plenty of privacy and would be able to talk. Missy had been working so hard lately, he could see the fatigue all over her still-gorgeous face.

Their delectable entrees arrived, along with a perfectly chilled bottle of crisp and fruity pinot grigio, and the keen-eyed detective observed his darling wife pushing her crab fettuccini around on her plate rather than eating it with her usual gusto.

"Okay, beautiful, tell me what's on your mind. I know that if you're not wolfing down your favorite pasta, there's clearly something wrong," he prompted gently, capturing her hand in his.

Her eyes filled with tears, but Missy blinked them back, leading Chas to believe that whatever she had to say might be worse than he thought.

"Oh Chas… I feel so terrible…" she began, looking down at the tablecloth.

"Why? What is it?" he brushed the back of her hand with his thumb.

"I just… I've been feeling a little bit overwhelmed lately, with baking and running the cupcake shop and trying to help out at the Inn when I can…"

"That's completely understandable, sweetie," he soothed, interrupting her. "It's okay to take a break every now and then, you know."

"I know… and that's kind of what I want to talk with you about," Missy raised her kitten-grey eyes to meet his.

"Whatever you need…"

She took a deep breath. "I hate to say this, after we've worked so hard… but…"

"But what?" he prodded gently.

"I think I might want to close *Cupcakes in Paradise*," she admitted, her eyes growing moist again.

"That's okay," he assured her, holding both her hands in his. "Whatever you need, sweetie. What's going on? Tell me what you're thinking."

Chas reached into the pocket of his sport coat and produced a linen handkerchief. Missy took it and blotted quickly at her eyes.

"It's just… we hardly have any time to spend together, and when I've been at the shop all day, I just get so tired. I could still bake for parties and occasions, but doing that and running the shop has just gotten to be too much. Is that awful of me to say?" she asked, her eyes large.

Her husband smiled fondly at her. "Not at all. I would love to have you around more, and I've noticed that you do seem tired. If you want to close the shop, close it. We can either sell it, or turn it into a guest cottage, since it backs up to the beach too," he shrugged.

"Oh, Chas, really? You're not disappointed in me for giving up?" Missy asked.

"Sweetie, you're not giving up, you're being smart and trying to do what's best for you… and for us. How could I be even the least bit upset about that?" He caressed her cheek with the back of his hand.

"Thank you," she threw her arms around his neck and kissed him soundly.

The detective chuckled, more than pleased at his wife's relief.

"Think you can manage a few more bites now?" he asked, glancing down at her nearly full plate.

"Yes, I'm suddenly starving," Missy grinned, picked up her fork and attacked the pasta with her usual enthusiasm.

Chapter 2

Fortunately, there had been no homicides in Calgon for a while, so Chas's morning had been consumed with catching up on paperwork and looking through evidence on several lesser crimes. When his stomach growled, reminding him that it was lunch time, he decided to visit Betsy's, a nearby diner, rather than traveling all the way home for his midday meal. He was happy to see that Phillip "Kel" Kellerman, a local, world-renowned artist, who just happened to be the fiancé of Missy's best friend Echo, bellied up to the counter, attacking a mountainous club sandwich with great gusto.

"Hey, Kel," the detective greeted his friend. "I haven't seen you around in a while."

"Chas," the artist replied, still chewing, but offering his hand. "I've been in New York. I had a showing there for a week—just got back yesterday."

"Good to see you," Chas nodded. "Mind if I join?"

"Not at all, I saved you a seat," Kel gestured to the empty chair next to him.

Betsy Boggus, the iron-haired, raspy-voiced owner of the place, came over, order pad in hand and pen poised.

"It's not every day that we get someone as handsome as you gracing our fair establishment," she chuckled. "What can I get you, Detective?"

"Whatever that colossal thing is that Kel has, with a cup of soup and a very large coffee," Chas grinned at the older woman.

Betsy had the best diner food in town, and ran her place like a benevolent dictator. She had her favorite customers—Kel and Chas were both on that list—and she treated them like kings. It was more than a bit coincidental that her favorites tended to be both talkative and good tippers. The artist and the detective had both benefitted at various times from the wealth of information that seemed to pass through the diner's doors, and Betsy could be counted on to keep an eye on her patrons, gleaning more from casual conversation and observation than some of the rookies on the force did with direct questioning.

"Anything interesting going on that I should know about?" was her nonchalant question to the men as she placed Chas's gargantuan sandwich platter down in front of him.

"Thankfully, no. Things are quiet for a change," the detective eyed his meal. "It's going to take me a couple of hours to work my way through that much food, Betsy," he grinned.

"Good thing you don't shy away from a challenge, Detective," she tossed back over her shoulder, heading to the kitchen. "Let me know if you need a to-go box."

"Must be nice to have a little down time," Kel observed, munching away at his lunch.

"Knock on wood," Chas nodded his enthusiastic agreement. "But I really want to take Missy away for a bit—maybe go see my family in upstate New York."

Kel put down his sandwich. "My grandfather used to own a resort in the Catskills. He sold it about forty years ago, with a provision that family members and guests could stay at no cost, in perpetuity. If you're really looking to get away, I can make arrangements for a couple of cabins and Echo and I could join you. Spencer too, if he wanted to tag along," the artist offered.

"That's a great idea," the detective agreed. "My dad had quite the antique and classic car collection that's housed on the family estate. The house and grounds have been opened to the public as a museum, but the cars were willed to me, so you, Spencer and I can take them out for a spin while the girls go to the spa or something," he suggested.

"I think we need to make this happen," Kel replied. "They've had a really warm spring up there, so it should be beautiful up in the mountains. You talk to Missy and Spencer, I'll talk to Echo, and let's do this."

"To vacation," Chas said, raising his chipped coffee mug in a toast.

"To vacation," Kel repeated, clinking the mugs together.

Chapter 3

Missy chattered excitedly with her best friend, former Californian and lifelong vegan, Echo Willis, in the back of the limousine that Chas had rented to take everyone to the airport in Miami, where they'd board a plane for New York. Since Kel had secured three luxury cabins for the group, Chas insisted on paying transportation expenses for everyone.

Though he was a detective, and a darn good one at that, Chas Beckett had inherited a fortune from his late father. He'd grown up in a wealthy family, but had always wanted to do something with his life that made a difference, so, after a very expensive Ivy League-education, he'd shocked the entire family by becoming a police officer, eventually working his way up to the rank of detective.

Chas was the only one of his siblings who had rejected a life of leisure, preferring to make his own way in the world, despite his healthy golden safety net. The only outward sign of his privileged origins was the way that he dressed. His fine fabric suits and shirts were exquisitely tailored and came from the finest design houses. His shoes, ties, watches, and accessories were top shelf, and he often changed into more casual attire before heading to a crime scene, keeping extra clothing in his office and the trunk of his car just in case.

What the rest of the group didn't know was that Chas had made first-class reservations for the entire trip. There were luxury seats reserved on the airplane, and a limousine would be waiting to pick them up on the other end and take them to the resort in the Catskills. It wasn't about being pretentious—because that was definitely not his style—it was about providing the most relaxing and enjoyable vacation experience possible.

The detective loved nothing more than seeing the smile on his lovely wife's face as she left the cares and concerns of daily life behind, and he exchanged a knowing glance with Spencer and Kel, when she and Echo, heads together, chattering like magpies in their spacious leather first-class seats, burst into laughter, Bloody Marys in hand.

The uniformed chauffeur spoke into the intercom in front of the tall iron gates that surrounded the exclusive Catskills resort, the Pinnacle, announcing the arrival of their party. The lock on the heavy gates disengaged with a metallic thunk and the doors rolled open. Further down the red brick roadway stood a guard shack, where two heavily armed guards stood watch, making certain that no unauthorized persons got behind the tall, razor-topped walls of the resort. There were more armed guards stationed at strategic points along the wall and around the grounds, because the safety and security of the celebrities, politicians, and other high-profile guests who vacationed there was paramount. There were multiple security centers on-site, where elite professionals watched security camera footage around the clock. It was said that kings, queens, and presidents had visited the esteemed resort, and the outside world never knew it.

Missy's eyes were wide as she took in the view outside of the luxuriously appointed limo. She was a bit intimidated by the level of security, and actually gasped out loud when she saw the main lodge of the Pinnacle, which closely resembled a medieval castle.

"Oh my goodness, is that where we're going to be staying?" she wondered, gripping Echo's arm.

Kel chuckled. "No, darling girl, that's where people who don't know the owners slum it. We have guest cottages with views of the lake that will take your breath away."

Spencer smiled and shook his head, and Missy blinked a couple of times, then returned to taking in the view. Missy's vision of "cottages" bore no resemblance to the reality of the massive luxury homes that backed up to a pristine, crystal-clear lake with private boat docks. Each 5000+ square feet "cottage" came with a housekeeper, a chef, and an enclosed golf cart for getting around the property. Guests could elect to have their staff stay on-site, or stand by to be summoned when needed. Since Missy and the gang were looking for an intimate, relaxing vacation, they would use minimal staff.

Spencer insisted that he be allowed to stay in the still-opulent staff quarters in the basement of Missy and Chas's cottage. Kel strongly felt that the Marine should have all of the benefits and luxuries as the rest of them, but finally accepted the young man's desire for much humbler surroundings, where he could be easily contacted by his employers... just in case.

Herb Finkelstein, grandson of the man who had bought the Pinnacle from Kel's grandfather, had greeted them personally at the main lodge upon their arrival, and had assured them that all of the vast resources of the resort were at their disposal—if there was anything at all that they wanted or needed, all they had to do was ask.

The main lodge was an enormous structure which housed guest rooms, a salon and spa, a theater, an impressive library, a massive indoor swimming pool, and state-of-the-art gym facilities, as well as a grand dining hall and gilded ballroom. There were social activities scheduled daily, and Missy and Echo were excited to discover that there was a nightly trivia competition in the main lounge.

"Thank you so much, Kel. This is going to be fun," Missy exclaimed, impulsively throwing her arms around the artist's neck and hugging him tightly.

"There's no one more deserving of a peaceful retreat, dear lady," he replied, hugging her back. "It's my pleasure."

While the vacationers were touring the stately lodge with their host, the housekeepers had unpacked and stowed their luggage, placing items neatly in closets and drawers. The group decided to freshen up and meet at the dining hall for dinner a couple of hours later, excited that their week of relaxation had officially begun.

Chapter 4

Echo was thrilled that the Pinnacle employed a full-time vegan chef for guests with those dietary preferences, and sat back in her chair, stuffed, after the best restaurant meal that she'd ever experienced.

"Oh my goodness… it's a good thing that they have a gym and personal trainers here. With food like this, I could easily go home twenty pounds heavier," she chuckled.

"Me too," Missy smiled and nodded. "We'll have to start our spa day tomorrow with a nice workout."

"We'll probably be on the road to my family's estate by then," Chas interjected. "It'll take us about an hour to get there, and I want to show Kel and Spencer around the house and take some of the cars out for a spin, so we'll meet up with you two for dinner. I asked our chef to prepare dinner for nine, because I've invited my brother and sister to join us. I hope no one minds."

"Oh darling, you know I always want you to be with your family when you can. I think it's wonderful. You boys just be careful when you're driving those cars," Missy admonished.

Spencer grinned. "I'll try to keep them in line for you, Mrs. B," he promised, flashing dimples that caught the attention of several young socialites in the dining hall.

"Thank you, Spencer, I'm glad there'll be a responsible adult with these two," she teased, glancing playfully at Chas and Kel. Kel raised his wine glass in reply and Chas merely grinned at his relaxed and beautiful wife.

Kel turned to look at Chas as the limousine pulled up in front of iron gates set in a towering brick wall that was grander, by far, than anything at the Pinnacle. Since the estate museum was open to the public, the gates stood open, the security guard in his well-appointed shack giving them a jaunty wave as they pulled on through.

"I'd heard of the Beckett estate when my family used to come up here for summers, but we were never in a position to rub elbows with people of your station," the artist mused, taking in the manicured gardens and imposing structure that awaited at the end of a beautifully meandering drive. The Beckett house made the Pinnacle look like a gardener's shack.

"You grew up here?" Kel asked, eyebrows raised.

"Until the moment I could leave, yes," Chas nodded, his thoughts far away.

"Estranged?"

The detective came back to the present, shaking his head. "No, not at all. My father was an amazing man, who encouraged me to be whatever I wanted to be, even though he would have preferred to have me overseeing the operations of his various enterprises. My brother and sister could never understand why I wanted to be my own man—why I wanted to try to make my own way in the world, but my mother…" he paused a moment, swallowing hard and staring out the window at his childhood home.

"She was the only one who always understood. She respected and supported my decision."

Spencer nodded imperceptibly, also seeming lost in thought.

"It'll be interesting to meet your family," Kel said, watching his friend for a reaction.

"Interesting? Definitely," Chas sighed. "Shall we?" he asked, as the limo glided to a stop in front of enormous stone steps that led into the mansion. The chauffeur opened the door and they piled out, waiting for Chas to lead the way.

The detective tucked a one-hundred-dollar bill into the donation box at the entrance, and made his way through the marbled foyer to an office just beyond. Inside the mahogany-lined room, polishing his spectacles, sat an ancient man wearing a tuxedo that was a duplicate to the one that he'd worn when Chas's tiny footsteps pitter-pattered through these stately halls. When the men appeared in the doorway, he hastily put the thick glasses on and his face registered immediate delight.

"Master Charles!" he exclaimed, with just a hint of a British accent, practically leaping from his chair to embrace the detective.

"It's good to see you, Chalmers," Chas replied, warmly returning the man's effusive greeting.

"It's been such a long time, but I assure you that I have taken diligent care of your home in your absence, sir," the faithful servant, who had been with the family for longer than Chas had been alive, asserted.

"I have no doubt, Chalmers. You've always done a fine job of looking out for my family," was the gracious reply.

Chas introduced Kel and Spencer, the first shaking the servant's hand, the second, locking eyes with him in a manner that would've been surprising to anyone who had noticed the interaction.

"Pleasure to meet you, Mr. Bengal," the servant greeted the Marine veteran.

"Likewise," Spencer nodded, appearing already to be familiar with the elderly man in front of him.

Chalmers had been the manservant for Chas's dad since before the detective was born, and had been tasked with overseeing the day-to-day operation of the estate, even after it became a museum.

"Perhaps Maggie could give the gentlemen a tour through the home while we discuss a few things?" Chalmers asked.

"Of course," Chas nodded. Chalmers pushed a button on his phone and the Irish maid who had taken care of Missy when she first visited with Chas, appeared as though by magic.

"Master Charles, it's so good to see ya," she bowed her head, the Irish brogue thick, delight at seeing Chas brightening her plain, ruddy features.

"You too, Maggie," the detective gave her an affectionate smile.

"Come on then, lads, let's take a walkabout," she beamed at Kel and Spencer.

"Do lead on, dear lady," Kel grinned at the maid, ever the gallant gentleman.

He and Spencer went on a tour of the lavish estate while Chas talked family business with Chalmers, and the three men regrouped at the fifty-stall antique and classic car garage, which housed an extensive collection, willed to Chas by his father. There were gleamingly perfect sedans, convertibles, roadsters, and more. Some of the vehicles were so rare that they were one of only a handful of their kind in the world. Kel and Spencer wandered along with Chas, listening to the history of some of their favorites among all of the fine machinery.

"Well, this is a bit of a dream come true," Kel whistled appreciatively. "This building alone would've made it hard to oust me from this lovely estate."

"It's a different world," Chas remarked. "One in which I'm not entirely comfortable. The only regret that I have about leaving when I did is that I didn't get to see my dad as often as I would've liked in his latter years."

"I think the once-a-month commute from Louisiana was pretty devoted," Spencer said quietly, his gaze running over the lines of the Rolls Royce Silver Shadow that he stood next to.

Chas gazed at him quizzically. He hadn't met Spencer

until he moved to Florida, and hadn't told the Marine about his father, so he wondered how the young man knew so much. Figuring that Missy must have said something, he shrugged off his surprise.

"I wish it could've been more, but there's no sense in dwelling in the past," the detective recovered, moving to run a hand over the gleaming fender of a champagne-colored roadster.

"So, are you gents ready to hit the road in one of these babies?" he gave them a lopsided grin.

"Sure, which one are we taking?" Kel asked, eyeing the collection.

"Well, I'm taking this little beauty," Chas replied, leaning against the roadster. "You two choose your own."

"Seriously?" Spencer's eyebrows shot up his forehead. "I thought you were just going to take us along for the ride."

"That was my impression as well," Kel's eyes gleamed with anticipation.

"What fun would that be?" the detective chuckled. "Pick one that you want to drive, and we'll head back to the Pinnacle. They're having a road race for charity this weekend, and we can show off some of the collection."

"The Kellerman Classic?" Kel exclaimed, surprised. "We used to love watching it every summer, but I never dreamed I'd actually participate."

"What's the Kellerman Classic?" Spencer asked.

"Well, it's called the Pinnacle Classic now," Chas replied. "It's a chance for classic car owners from around the country to come showcase their favorites. Guests at the resort and people from surrounding communities come to watch. All of the proceeds go to charity—it's a yearly event," he explained.

"This little gal," the detective lightly patted the fender of the car that he was leaning against. "Is one of only three of this model and color left in the world."

"That sounds expensive," Spencer commented, eyeing the Rolls next to him.

"Dear boy, that car is worth more than the net worth of most people staying at the Pinnacle," Kel said, gazing appreciatively at the sleek vehicle.

"Wow. It looks like something I saw in a James Bond movie once."

"The car in the Bond movie was mocked-up to look like this one," Chas grinned. "But this girl doesn't swim, fly, or shoot; she just purrs."

"I don't know if I feel comfortable driving a car that costs more than I'll ever make in my lifetime," Spencer admitted with a shrug.

"Then choose one that's not as rare," Chas suggested. "Kel, what's your pick?"

"The red speedster, of course," the artist's eyes lit up as he headed toward the cherry bomb.

"Keys are in the glove box, and the button on the arm rest will raise the bay door," the detective instructed, climbing into his spymobile. "Spencer, just get in one and drive it," he encouraged. "Kel and I will lead the way." He opened his bay and revved the supercharged engine, guiding the vehicle out to the drive in front of the garage.

Spencer watched Chas head down a back drive that ultimately looped around to the front of the mansion, with Kel following closely behind. The bays had sensors that automatically closed the doors after the cars cleared the doorway. Realizing that he'd be left behind if he didn't choose a car and follow his boss, he jumped into the Silver Shadow, grabbed the keys out of the glove box, started the engine, guided the grand car gracefully out of its stall, and fell in behind the two sports cars.

Chapter 5

Spencer caught up easily to Kel, who was a safe distance behind Chas as they headed down the private drive toward the exit. Once the guard waved them through the gates, the pace changed dramatically, as Chas accelerated rapidly, letting the horses under the little car's hood do their job, with Kel right on his tail and Spencer cruising sedately some distance behind. The winding roads of the Catskills provided a fantastic course upon which to test the speed and handling of the exotic cars, and Chas took full advantage of the opportunity to see what the car could do, passing the few cars that he encountered like they were standing still and accelerating into the twists and turns like he was being chased by a rabid pack of demons. Kel, who apparently had a competitive streak in his artistic soul that no one had imagined, stayed closer to Chas's bumper than was probably prudent.

The mountain roads were a blast, and the weather was beautiful for a drive. Kel had pulled back the top on his convertible, and Chas and Spencer had all of their windows down, delighting in the spring breeze. The champagne roadster came screaming around a turn at breakneck speed, and Kel saw an opportunity to pull ahead. Putting the pedal of the cherry bomb to the floor, he zoomed into the oncoming lane to go around Chas. The detective saw him beginning to pass in his rearview mirror, and hit the gas himself, intending to defeat the artist's intentions of getting ahead. He grinned from ear to ear as his champagne beauty shot forward.

Kel accelerated again, determined to pass his friend, and the two cars made a nearly hairpin turn, almost side by side. Kel inched forward, confident that he was finally going to be able to take the lead, when a semi came around the corner barreling right toward him. Chas, concentrating on holding his position, didn't see the semi immediately, and continued to accelerate, leaving Kel stuck in the oncoming lane.

When the detective glanced up again, he saw the semi and applied the brakes, as did Kel, leaving the two cars still side by side, with the artist directly in the path of the oncoming semi, who was now honking his horn frantically. Guided by instinct rather than thought, Chas hit the gas pedal hard, shooting ahead of Kel, who braked more firmly and swerved in behind the champagne car at the last second, missing Chas's bumper by mere inches, as the irate trucker thundered past.

Spencer had been behind the two of them the entire time, and expelled his breath in a relieved rush when Kel fell back into place behind Chas. Their fearless leader continued the rest of the way at a much more sedate speed, and the artist elected not to challenge him again. Spencer heaved a sigh of relief, as he'd been nearly certain that he was going to be picking up the pieces of two friends and a couple of very expensive cars.

Missy and Echo reclined in heated massage chairs, dressed in fluffy white robes. The friends had mud on their faces, cucumbers on their eyes, and their hands were wrapped in bags of paraffin.

"Oh my goodness, it's been so long since we've been able to just get away from it all and relax," Echo sighed happily. "It was so amazing of Maggie to offer to run the candle shop for me while we're gone."

"Well, since we didn't have any guests scheduled for the Inn this week, our awesome innkeeper was more than willing to keep busy with the candle shop. She loves the scents," Missy replied.

Echo had begun making candles scented like Missy's cupcake flavors, to sell in *Cupcakes in Paradise*; the handcrafted candles had become so popular with both tourists and locals that demand had exploded. She'd been able to quickly save enough money to open up a shop of her own in a quaint little building downtown.

"It's nice that Spencer is getting a vacation too," the candle maker commented drowsily.

"I agree. He works so hard at the Inn and shop, he deserves a break. I can't help but think that he's probably acting as a bit of a babysitter for Chas and Kel today, though," she chuckled. If only she knew…

A slim, young, and, aristocratic, auburn-haired woman, who had just entered and was sitting in a massage chair next to Missy, looked up in surprise.

"I'm sorry, I couldn't help but overhear your conversation," she said, gazing at Missy wide-eyed. "But… you said Chas. Are you talking about Chas Beckett?"

Missy and Echo were startled at the realization that someone had overheard their conversation, and both sat up, removing the cucumbers from their eyes.

"Chas is my husband," Missy smiled, curious. "Do you know him?" she asked, thinking that the young woman looked vaguely familiar.

"Oh… well, we knew each other when I was little," the redhead faltered a bit. "We played tennis at the same club."

"Oh, how nice," Missy replied, wondering at the younger woman's nervous demeanor. "What's your name?"

"Muffy. Muffy Fairchild," she gave Missy a tight smile.

"Well, it's nice to meet you, Muffy. I'm Missy, and this is my friend Echo."

"Pleasure," Muffy smiled faintly, looking uncomfortable.

Fortunately, the women were saved from any further attempts at awkward conversation by the arrival of the spa attendants who came in to finish Missy and Echo's facials.

Chapter 6

"You look amazing," Chas kissed his coiffed, pedicured, and pampered wife soundly when he, Spencer, and Kel met up with Missy and Echo after their gender-traditional afternoons.

"Well, thank you. I don't want your brother and sister to think that you've married a ragamuffin," she smiled up at him.

"You know how much I care about what my brother and sister think," the detective made a face.

"Honey, you're lucky to have a brother and sister," she reminded her husband wistfully. Her only sister had died several years earlier. "Enjoy them, despite their... idiosyncrasies."

Chas sighed, but gazed fondly at his tender-hearted mate. "I'll try," he nodded, thinking about how very different he was from his siblings.

His brother Reginald had been more than content to play the part of international playboy, spending his trust fund as though it was limitless; and his sister Olivia had married well, but seemed miserable. Chas had faithfully visited his ailing father, traveling at least once a month from his home in LaChance, Louisiana, to the opulent nursing facility in upstate New York where the elder Beckett lived; but the other two had rarely bothered to even make an appearance, despite living less than an hour away.

"When we were at the spa today, we met someone who knew you."

"That's not terribly surprising," Chas remarked with a smile. "Quite a few families that were around when I used to come here with my family are still making an appearance. Especially during the Pinnacle Classic. I've run into several guys that I went to college with who are here to show off their cars."

"You're not thinking of racing are you?" Missy asked, her eyes wide with concern.

"It's not really a race, sweetie," he assured her, tracing a finger under her chin. "There's a track that runs around the property, and guys who want to drive their favorite cars around for the tourists donate to a designated charity for that privilege. It's all in good fun."

"Which means that you *are* going to participate." Missy couldn't hide her concern.

"I am. As is Kel, and we're going to be perfectly fine," Chas pulled her into his arms. "Let's get ready for dinner."

Dinner at Chas and Missy's "cottage" went surprisingly well. Reggie tried to capture Echo's attention until he discovered that she was engaged, and Livvy made some catty remarks about her being vegan, but the feisty chandler put her firmly in her place, much to the delight of the social maven's younger brothers.

The chef and servers presented the group with a delicious meal, and once a bit of wine had been served with the appetizers, everyone lightened up and enjoyed themselves. Spencer, taking careful note of the family dynamic, made certain to keep a still mildly bristling Olivia engaged in conversation about her tennis game, her golf scores, the country club, and anything else that made her feel better about herself, much to Chas's relief.

"You going to let me enter one of your beauties in the Classic tomorrow, old boy?" Reggie asked his elder brother, taking a huge gulp of wine.

"Not a chance, Reg. I know how you drive, and there's a reason that Father left the collection to me," the detective replied without batting an eye.

"Well, you may have been the favorite, but I've had more fun," the playboy smirked, leaning back in his chair.

"We have very different definitions of fun," Chas sipped his wine, giving Missy a glance that made her blush.

"Eww… I'm going to leave before this conversation gets any worse," Olivia announced. "Spencer, would you mind escorting me out? You never know who might be lurking in the bushes," she asked, clearly loving the attention of the much-younger veteran.

"It'd be my pleasure, ma'am," the Marine stood, excusing himself and offering his arm to Chas's sister.

"Are you two going to plan on attending the Classic tomorrow?" Chas asked, before Livvy made it to the door.

"Heavens no," his sister wrinkled her delicate nose. "All that noise and the smell, plus being surrounded by the unwashed masses... no thank you. We'll have lunch at the club before you go, Chas. Melissa, it was lovely to see you again," she waved breezily in Missy's direction. Missy stood up to give her sister-in-law a hug, but the woman was gone before she could make it to the other side of the table.

"I'll be there, sport. If for no other reason than to critique your driving," Reggie announced smugly, rising from his chair to give Missy the hug that she'd missed from their sister, lingering long enough that Chas stood as well.

"Some things never change," the detective muttered with a thin smile.

He shook Reggie's hand, and walked his brother to the door, making certain that he had a driver, because there was no way in the world that he'd let him drive home, after the copious amount of fine French wine that the younger man had consumed.

Spencer was heading back up the steps to the porch, when Chas and Reggie came out, and the detective placed a hand on the Marine's arm. The young veteran stayed on the porch while Reginald Beckett climbed clumsily into the back of the waiting limo.

"I saw what you did in there. Thank you," Chas said simply, raising a hand to wave as his brother's limo pulled away.

"I don't know what you mean, sir. I was just entertaining a pretty lady," Spencer grinned, knowing exactly what the detective meant.

Chas chuckled and clapped him on the back. "Whatever. I owe you a beer," he promised as they headed back inside.

Chapter 7

"You're sure that you don't want to take a spin around with us?" Chas asked Spencer, pulling on his driving gloves. "I'll take care of the donation."

"Nah, I'm good," the Marine replied. "Somebody has to keep the ladies company in the good seats," he joked. "Good luck to you both, though."

Chas and Kel thanked him, and the young man headed out of the lineup area, moving past classic, antique, and exotic cars of every color and stripe. Some of the participants clearly were there for the adrenaline rush of trying to pull ahead of the pack, while others were content to preen like peacocks, strutting about the track in their perfectly polished vehicles. Kel was intent upon testing his driving skills against the other roadster drivers, whereas Chas was merely out to enjoy a few leisurely laps around the track.

Spencer stopped short when he came upon a car that looked just like the one that Chas was driving.

"I can certainly appreciate you stopping to gawk at this fine beast, dear boy. She's only one of three left in the world," an older man in a jaunty herringbone cap remarked, amused at Spencer's expression.

"And two of them are here… figure the odds," the Marine replied, not at all rattled by the older gentleman's mockery.

"Really?" the thought seemed to stop the man in his tracks. "I honestly thought that no one but I would be bold enough to drive an asset like this in a somewhat public venue."

"Asset?"

"Yes, of course. While this lovely car is appreciated for her performance and appearance, she's also worth quite a pretty penny. Last year, when the fourth that was in existence was totaled by a drunken sot who didn't have enough sense to use a driver, the value of the remaining three nearly quadrupled."

"Wow, so one man's misfortune led to an increased value for three others?"

"That's how these type of assets work, dear boy," the man shrugged, and proceeded to ignore him while polishing an imaginary spot on the fender with a special cloth.

Closer to the front of the lineup, Spencer saw yet another car that was identical to the one that Chas was driving, marveling that there were only three of them left in the world, and all of them had somehow ended up here. He headed for the box seats that were awarded to a handful of special guests at the resort, while those who had purchased tickets to come in and watch the spectacle stood at the fence that surrounded the track.

The yearly charitable event was a logistical nightmare for the top-notch security team that was tasked with protecting high-profile guests at the resort. Every team member would be serving multiple shifts until the event was over, and every last non-guest had been politely escorted from the stately grounds. There were extra personnel manning the wall around the resort, and plenty of heavily armed ladies and gentlemen in suits who circulated among the guests during the event.

Spencer took his front row seat with Missy, Echo, and Chas's brother Reggie, accepting a tall glass of iced tea from a server. The day was cool, but not chilly, and the sun shone brightly on the early spring day. After a few minutes, the participants' engines revved, indicating the imminent start of the race. When the flag lowered, allowing the pack to surge onto the track, some cars flew by, while others set a more sedate pace.

The Marine saw the first car that looked like Chas's take off as though it were jet-propelled. The second look-alike came flying out of the gate as well, while Chas came out more slowly, but still faster than many of the cars around him. The pack rounded the first corner, with the sporty models taking the lead and the sedans trailing behind in a dignified stroll. The crowd gasped, and Spencer stood when he saw a car that looked like Chas's go careening from the track, slamming into a towering sugar maple to land with an eardrum-shattering crash of metal and glass.

A collection of cars swerved, slammed on the brakes, and eventually came to a halt past the horrific incident, while the cars in the front continued on, completely unaware that they'd lost one of their own. Spencer placed both hands on the top of the fence separating him from the track and vaulted over it, taking off for the wreckage in a dead run as Missy and Echo stood watching in horror.

"That wasn't Chas's car, was it?" Missy whispered, clinging to her best friend.

"I don't know," Echo shook her head as both women fixed their gaze on the smoke that was beginning to rise from the site of the crash.

Spencer was still several hundred yards away from the balled-up metal remains of the car, when he saw its license plate and verified, to his profound relief, that the car didn't belong to his boss, but unfortunately to the older gentleman that he had met not half an hour ago. He scanned the parking lot of cars on the track behind him, as an ambulance and fire truck whipped past, and saw Chas heading toward him.

"You okay?" he asked, trotting over to his boss.

"Fine. How bad is it?" the detective glanced toward the mangled car, which was shielded from view, surrounded by first responders who were trying to extricate the driver.

"I didn't get close, but it doesn't look good," Spencer replied grimly.

"I wonder who it was," Chas said quietly as the two men headed closer to the scene.

"Older guy. I met him after I left you, before the race."

"Great dresser? Rather biting sense of humor?"

"Yep, that's the guy," the Marine nodded. "You know him?"

"I knew of him. He offered to buy my father's car collection after the funeral. I refused, obviously, and he seemed quite bent out of shape about it. Didn't seem like a bad guy, though," Chas explained with a sigh, shaking his head.

Their conversation was cut short by the repeated blaring of a golf cart horn, cutting through the crowd and headed right for them. Aboard the tiny vehicle were Missy, Echo, and Reggie. The cart had scarcely come to a stop before Missy leaped from it, making a beeline for her husband.

"I was so worried," she blurted, throwing her arms around his neck.

"I'm okay, sweetie," Chas assured her, while Spencer thanked Reggie for bringing the golf cart out onto the track so that Missy could get to her husband.

"Where's Kel?" Echo asked softly, her face white.

No one had to answer when the artist came jogging over, picking up his fiancée and hugging her tight.

"Chas, I'm so sorry. I tried to steer away from all of the traffic, but I got sideswiped by the diamond-finish Mercedes. It's definitely fixable, but your cherry bomb has more than its share of diamond sparkle at the moment," Kel explained ruefully.

"No worries," Chas squeezed his shoulder. "I'm just glad that you're okay. Reggie, go ahead and take Kel and the girls back to the cottages. Spencer and I are going to see if there's anything that we can do," the detective instructed.

"Be careful," Missy cautioned, kissing her husband gratefully before heading back to the golf cart.

Chapter 8

A somber mood permeated the resort after the crash that killed Judge Ian Gordon. The crowds of spectators had been ushered out quietly, and the entire area had been roped off while crews investigated the wreckage and cleaned up the debris. Missy and Chas were sipping coffee on their back porch, each wrapped up in their own thoughts, when their housekeeper came out, clearing her throat to get their attention.

"Pardon the interruption, sir," she addressed Chas politely. "But there's a gentleman at the front door to see you."

Chas and Missy looked at each other, surprised.

"Is it my brother?" the detective asked, setting his coffee mug on the wicker table next to his chair.

"No sir. It's a Detective Wallace Charlton."

Chas grimaced. He and Charlton had gone through the police academy together, and Charlton made a point to mock his Ivy League-educated classmate at every turn. He'd been bitter about Chas's privileged upbringing and jealous of the stellar progression of his career.

"Thank you. I'll be right there," he dismissed the housekeeper.

"What's this about?" Missy asked, reaching for her husband's hand.

"I'll find out. Nothing to worry about, I'm sure," he soothed, kissing her lightly before disappearing through the french doors leading into the cottage.

"Wallace," Chas greeted the detective, extending his hand politely.

"Beckett," Charlton responded, ignoring the outstretched hand.

Chas raised an eyebrow at the man's rudeness, and dropped his hand. "What can I do for you?"

"I need to speak with you for a few minutes. May I come in?" the detective asked, his expression just two shades shy of being overtly hostile.

"No. I'm here on vacation with my wife. If you need to speak with me about something, we can do that on the porch," Chas replied firmly, stepping outside and indicating that Wallace could have a seat across from him, on an elegant wrought iron chair.

The detective might have valid reasons for his visit, but after behaving so rudely, the conversation would take place on Chas's terms.

"You up here visiting family?" Charlton asked, a bit too casually, after taking his seat.

"None of your business, Wallace. Let's get to the point, shall we? Why are you here?"

The bitter detective sat forward, and eyed Chas with a predatory glare.

"Actually, your reasons for being here might end up being quite relevant," Charlton bit out. "Judge Ian Gordon was murdered, and you know as well as I do that there was more than a little bit of animosity between you and his Honor," he sneered. "If you had anything to do with the judge's death, it won't matter how many billions your daddy left you, you'll be going to jail."

"Let's get one thing straight, Charlton," Chas began, deadly calm. "You don't come to me with threats and accusations that'll get you nowhere but in some very hot water when you're proved wrong. I have nothing to say to you, but I will be having a conversation with your chief as soon as you get out of my sight, which needs to be sooner rather than later. Am I being clear?"

Wallace Charlton's eyes narrowed to slits and a vein pulsed on his forehead. He leaned toward Chas in what could be considered a menacing manner, and was about to speak, when a shadow passed over them, catching their attention.

"Is there a problem here?" Spencer Bengal, Marine veteran, asked quietly, having appeared out of thin air.

Charlton sat back and shook his head.

"You've got hired goons taking care of you now? Makes you wonder why a man who isn't doing anything wrong would hire protection. What are you afraid of, Beckett?" he snarled, mocking.

Spencer glanced at Chas, who continued to stare down the ill-mannered detective.

"This man is a member of my family," Chas replied, his eyes locked on Wallace's. "I don't need protection, and I'd be happy to prove that to you by personally escorting you from the premises if you're not gone in the next few seconds." He rose to his feet and towered over the smaller man, who suddenly seemed much less confident.

Wallace slid his chair back and stood, faltering under the watchful gaze of his career rival and the ever-vigilant Marine. He started to speak but seemed to think better of it and turned to go.

"How much did you hear?" Chas asked Spencer, when the surly detective's car had disappeared down the private drive.

"Enough. You want me to get Kel and the ladies home?"

The detective shook his head. "If there's been a murder, none of the guests will be allowed to check out until they've been questioned. I'm going to call the chief and see what they've got. In the meantime, keep an eye out for anything suspicious. If there's a killer in the resort, we don't know who he might target next, or if this was something personal between him and the judge."

Spencer nodded. "Will do."

Chas's cell phone buzzed, indicating that a text had come in, and when he read the message, he frowned, his forehead creasing.

"Bad news?"

"There was an attempted break-in at the museum," the detective replied. "I'm going to go check it out, and then pay a visit to the chief in person. I'd appreciate it if you held down the fort here."

"You got it, sir," Spencer agreed without hesitation.

Chapter 9

Missy had been up late, baking a new cupcake that she'd created after hearing that Chas had been questioned regarding the murder of Judge Gordon. Inspired by the sugar maple trees dotting the mountain slopes of the resort, she'd come up with a new maple custard cupcake that had the entire cottage smelling like the world's best breakfast.

She, Echo, and Kel sat down to their customary morning coffee and cupcake chat while Spencer went for a jog. Chas slept in after being up for much of the night talking with the police chief regarding the attempted break-in at his father's estate and the murder of the judge.

"I was really hoping that we could get away from crime and death and drama on this vacation," Missy mourned, picking apart a luscious cupcake topped with fluffy maple buttercream.

"Well, the sooner we figure out precisely what happened, and who killed that poor man, the sooner we'll be able to get back to the business of relaxation," Kel pointed out, optimistically.

"We've been pretty good at solving these things in the past," Echo added. "Let's put our heads together and do this."

"But we don't know anyone up here. Even Kel doesn't have many contacts," Missy reminded them.

"Melissa Gladstone-Beckett, I've never known you to shy away from a challenge," Kel scolded gently, taking a huge bite of his cupcake.

Missy smiled, knowing it was true, and dove right in.

"Okay, so, after talking to Chas, here's what we know so far: the brake line in the judge's car was cut just before the race. A puddle of brake fluid in the staging area backs that up."

"So, whoever did this had access to the staging area," Echo mused.

"Which means it had to have been a guest, or part of the Pinnacle staff, because spectators weren't allowed in the staging area," Kel finished for her.

"Exactly," Missy nodded. "So that narrows it down to a few hundred people. How on earth are we going to figure out who did this?"

"We have to find out who might have a reason to eliminate Judge Gordon," Kel replied, pursing his lips.

"And how are we going to do that?" Echo asked.

"Let me do some digging. There should be plenty of public records available that will allow us to see who might have reason to be homicidally upset with one of his decisions," the artist stood, heading back to his cottage for his laptop.

"Good idea. In the meantime, Echo and I are going to keep our eyes open for anything that seems suspicious," Missy called after him.

The two women sat in silence, drinking their coffee and nibbling on cupcakes for no more than a few seconds when Kel came back in.

"Dear lady, you're going to want to wake up Chas and come see this," he said, looking pale and gesturing toward the front porch.

Missy and Echo exchanged a startled glance, then Echo followed Kel to the porch while Missy went to rouse Chas from his slumber.

"What is this, and why is it here?" Missy asked, peering down at what looked like a strange set of cooking shears.

Chas exchanged a knowing glance with Kel and replied.

"They're bolt cutters," he explained. "And if I had to guess, I'd bet that they are the very ones that were used on the judge's car."

"What makes you say that?" Echo asked, bending down over the cutters.

"See that dab of fluid smeared near the cut points?" he pointed with the tip of a pen. "Dollars to donuts, it's brake fluid."

"But how did they get here?" Missy asked, eyes wide, scanning the area around them as though she expected someone to jump out of the bushes at any moment.

"Someone is trying to frame Chas," Kel observed, not bothering to mince words.

"Which means that we have to figure out who the killer is, because the police will be looking at Chas," Echo commented practically.

"No," the detective shook his head. "You all are going to stay safe by staying out of this. I've already texted the police chief. He's on his way over, and will collect this to process it for fingerprints and find out if the residue actually is brake fluid. Wallace Charlton may be a less-than-ideal detective, but the chief is a good guy. He'll get to the bottom of this."

A look passed between Missy and Echo that clearly conveyed their intention to keep digging, no matter what Chas said.

"Well then," Kel said, breaking up a silence that felt a bit strained. "I'll be heading back to the cottage. Let's regroup for lunch, yes?"

"You three can. I'm going to be pretty busy," Chas sighed.

Spencer Bengal ran hard on the trails that crisscrossed the sometimes thickly forested areas of the resort. Feeling the hair on the back of his neck raise just a bit, he slowed his pace, listening and scanning the wooded areas ahead and to his sides. He didn't see anyone, but felt someone or something watching him. Senses attuned, on full alert, the Marine stopped jogging and leaned against a tree, pretending to stretch out his muscles and taking the time for a good hard look through the brush. He heard nothing but the breath moving in and out of his lungs and his own heartbeat keeping blood thrumming through his veins, but he felt an undeniable presence, and then he knew.

"You on vacation too?" he asked, without bothering to turn around. He knew who was behind him now.

"I don't even know what vacation is," Janssen drawled, taking a toothpick out of his mouth and flicking it into the pine needles surrounding the tree under which he sat calmly, as though he belonged.

"Clearly, you've identified some holes in the Pinnacle's state-of-the-art security systems," Spencer remarked, turning to face his fellow veteran with a wry smile. Janssen had shown up multiple times in Florida, and had helped Spencer keep his adopted family of Missy and the gang safe on more than one occasion.

"Yeah, these boys ain't too bad. Better'n most actually, but,... you know how it is. In like a deer, out like a fox," Janssen shrugged, a corner of his scarred mouth quirking upward in a half-smile.

"What are you doing up this far north? Thought you were wintering down in Florida?" Spencer crossed his arms and leaned back on the tree that he'd been using as a stretching post.

"I could ask you the same question," the other war-toughened young man replied easily.

"I go where the family goes."

Janssen gave him a long look. "Family," he nodded. "That kind of thinking can be dangerous, you know. Clouds the issue."

"I'll take my chances," Spencer shrugged.

"You know you could get recognized up here."

Spencer bent over to touch his toes. "That can happen anywhere. I keep my eyes open. I have a feeling that there's more going on here than any of the jet set realizes," he said grimly.

Janssen nodded. "I've got your back, but we're going to get picked up by the sensors that I put offline pretty soon, so we'd best split up for now," he said, rising to his feet and dusting the pine needles from the back of his jeans.

"You staying around here?"

"Define 'around.'" The scarred man grinned and disappeared into the deepest parts of the forest as Spencer headed back to the cottage.

Chapter 10

Spencer had some downtime during the afternoon while Chas met with the chief of police and Missy, Kel, and Echo went down to the main lodge to play trivia, trying to take their mind off of the recent morbid series of events. Dressed in all-white tennis gear, Spencer slung a racquet over his shoulder and planned to revisit the staging area for the Pinnacle Classic, right near the tennis courts.

Crossing to the cement pad where the cars had waited to enter the track, he quickly located the puddle of brake fluid staining the surface. He scanned the area around the pad looking for any sort of clue that might have been left behind, and realized that he wasn't alone.

"Hi!" a slim, leggy redhead about his age, greeted him. "Looking for something?" she asked.

Spencer flashed his legendary dimples, hoping to distract her. He didn't really understand why women found him attractive, but he did occasionally use that fact to his advantage.

"Yeah. I lost a ball over here somewhere. You'd think I'd be able to find a bright yellow ball more easily," he shook his head.

"Oh. I just came from the courts, I didn't see anyone over there," she looked at him curiously.

"I hadn't actually made it over to the courts yet, I was bouncing the ball on my racquet and got a little carried away," he shrugged sheepishly.

"Might have gone a bit better for you if you'd taken the cover off of your racquet," the redhead observed, looking as though she was stifling a laugh.

"Oh, it was off. I put it back on when I started looking around. You don't walk around with your cover off, do you?" he pretended to be taken aback by the thought.

"No. Of course not. My racquet is back at the court," she explained. "I could use an opponent if you're up for it," she smiled prettily, and Spencer had to remind himself to stay focused on his task.

"I'd love a game, but you have to promise to go easy on me, I'm a little rusty," the Marine grinned wickedly.

"No promises," was the mischievous reply. "I'm Muffy," she extended a well-manicured hand, which he engulfed in his.

"Spencer."

"Nice to meet you, Spencer. Ready to play?"

"Definitely," he nodded, working hard not to show how distracted he was by a figure lurking in the edge of the forest that bordered the tennis courts on one side.

Judging by the height and build, Spencer guessed it was a man who was trying to hide but wasn't very adept at it. Spencer wondered absently if Janssen would have a little chat with whoever it was, while he played tennis with the delicate socialite in front of him. He had hoped that he wouldn't encounter anyone, but since he had, he needed to follow through on looking like just another guest so that he wouldn't arouse suspicion.

"Where are the rest of your balls?" she asked innocently.

"I beg your pardon?" Spencer was momentarily caught off guard, watching the lurking presence in his peripheral vision.

"You said that you lost the one that you were playing with, but you don't seem to have any others with you."

"Oh, right. Yeah, I don't typically lose them, so I only brought the one," he shrugged, hoping that she bought the lame excuse.

"Confident, aren't you?" she grinned. "That's okay, I have extras, we can use mine."

The Marine was more than a bit surprised and impressed at the ferocity with which the woman attacked the game. When they finished, sweaty and tired in a most satisfying way, he had won two out of their three games. Muffy brushed damp tendrils of coppery hair away from her forehead with a monogrammed towel and smiled at him with admiration.

"Great game," she nodded at him with obvious pleasure. "Next time I won't go so easy on you," she teased.

"Pretty and merciful too, that's a nice combination."

"Oh, please, I'm anything but pretty at the moment, unless you're into sweaty, unkempt ladies," she protested, clearly loving the compliment.

"There's a certain charm in that," he tilted his head as if he were appraising her.

"I need hydration. Want to cool down with me at the juice bar?" Muffy offered, catching her lower lip between her teeth in a way artfully designed to look shy and fetching.

Seeing right through the ploy, he agreed nonetheless, and followed her to the small building behind the courts which housed a juice and smoothie bar. The pair sat down with their designer bottled waters and a couple of tropical concoctions that looked like they should have alcohol and a paper umbrella in them.

"I've seen you before, you know," Muffy remarked, sipping her drink.

"Oh?" Spencer's reply was mild, but internally, his system went on full alert.

"Yes," she nodded. "It's not often that we see tattoos around here, so it made me notice you. That and the fact that you look like you just stepped out of the pages of *GQ* magazine."

Some of the tension eased out of the Marine.

"Stop, you're making me blush," he chuckled, not even close to blushing. He'd heard similar lines so many times before that it was somewhat irritating, but at least he hadn't really been recognized, for which he was thankful.

"You're here with the Becketts, right? It's a shame what happened with them," she shook her head sadly.

"I'm afraid I don't know what you mean," Spencer's eyes narrowed slightly, but he maintained a pleasant smile.

"Well, I mean… you know, the judge being killed. The police are chasing after Charles pretty hard from what I've heard," she batted her eyes at him.

"Do you always believe everything that you hear?" the Marine replied easily, sipping his drink.

"Of course not, but in this case it makes sense. Charles was pretty rude to the judge when the poor old man asked to buy his father's car collection, and he's been estranged from his family for years. I don't know how well you know him, but he's not exactly the nicest person in the world."

"And you know all of this how?" Spencer assumed a slightly amused air so that she'd keep talking.

"Can you keep a secret?" she asked, leaning in.

"To the grave," he promised with mock-solemnity, making a crisscross motion over his heart, and leaning in as well, in an attempt to disarm her with proximity.

"I know that Charles Beckett is an awful person because he was engaged to my older sister, Amanda. He broke her heart and then left New York to go to some awful hick town down south," she confided in a voice just above a whisper, looking around as though she didn't want to be overheard.

"I hadn't heard that," the Marine feigned surprise, having heard the actual story, which was quite different from the version that Muffy had told.

"See what I mean? He puts on this humble, responsible façade, and really, he's just awful. I think that the police are probably on the right track. I hope you two aren't close," she cooed, her voice dripping with false sympathy.

"Nope, I just work for him," Spencer shrugged. "I hardly know him at all."

"He brought one of his staff with him?" she drew back in shock.

"I saved him from drowning, so the trip was kind of a reward."

Muffy suddenly seemed even more interested in him than she had before.

"Well, how very brave of you," she drawled, tracing a finger down his bicep.

Spencer saw a human-sized shadow flit past a window outside of the juice bar, and wondered if it was merely a coincidence.

Chapter 11

Detective Chas Beckett reviewed the videotape that Chalmers had set aside for him, of the attempted break-in at his family's estate. The footage was dark and grainy, but was clear enough to see that the figure who had been trying to get in was short and slight. The intruder had climbed partially up the wall before sensors detected him and security lights came blazing on, whiting out the picture on the cameras. The culprit had then run back toward the main road, heading south.

Chas surveyed the area carefully, looking for clues, and found a small footprint near the base of the wall where the intruder had climbed up. The print had most likely been made when the culprit jumped down from the wall and took off running. The detective took photos and measurements of the print and headed toward the main road in a southerly direction. He found a few more prints in the soft earth that told him he was headed in the right direction; when he reached the road, roughly a mile away from the breach point, he found two tire impressions in the ground near the shoulder, which he also photographed.

According to the police chief, there had been no fingerprints found on the bolt cutters that had been planted at Chas's cottage, which meant either that they'd been wiped down or—more likely—that whoever had placed them there had worn gloves. Of course, that made Detective Wallace Charlton suspect Chas even more, because he would know enough about crime scene investigation to not leave fingerprints.

What the detective didn't seem to want to accept was that if Chas had actually committed the crime and wiped down the murder weapon, he wouldn't have been careless enough to bring it home with him and leave it on his front porch. Beckett knew a setup when he saw one, and was determined to find the real killer.

"So, what did you find out?" Missy asked Kel impatiently when she and Echo sat down with the artist for coffee and cupcakes.

"Apparently, Judge Gordon was more than well-respected when it came to his rulings. He's from old money, like just about everyone else up here, and went into law simply for the joy of it," he shrugged.

"So, there weren't any rulings where someone might have wanted to take revenge?" Echo demanded. "How is that possible?"

"I didn't say that. I just said that they weren't easy to find. I did find one rather interesting connection though, particularly when one considers that Chas is the one being framed in this case," he announced.

"Out with it already!" Missy exclaimed, her stomach in knots.

"You're familiar with Amanda Heatherington, I presume," the artist began.

"Amanda Heatherington?" the color rose in Missy's face, but she took a breath, controlling her reaction.

"Yes, I'm familiar with her. She wanted to marry Chas, so killed her husband to try to make herself available for Chas, then attempted to kill me," she recounted, her blood boiling. "Why, what does she have to do with all of this? She's in prison."

"Did Judge Gordon put her there?" Echo chimed in, patting her agitated friend's hand absently.

Kel nodded. "Not only did he put her there, but a few months ago, her little sister was arrested for destruction of property, after crashing her little sports car into the side of a bar and grill, and he gave her one of the worst possible sentences for a well-heeled socialite."

"What's that?" Echo was intrigued.

"Community service," the artist revealed with an ironic chuckle. "She had to help out by serving meals in a homeless shelter."

"So, why are Amanda and her little sister significant?" Missy asked, losing patience.

"Amanda is significant because of her connection with Chas, and her little sister is significant because she's here."

"Amanda Heatherington's little sister is here at the resort? Do we know her? Have we seen her?" Echo demanded.

"I don't know. Her name is Muffy Fairchild. As you know, Heatherington was Amanda's married name," Kel replied.

The color drained from Missy's face and Echo clutched her hand as the two women exchanged a glance.

"What?" Kel asked, alarmed by the expressions on the women's faces.

"We met Muffy at the spa," Missy replied numbly. "We were talking about being on vacation and mentioned Chas's name. She said that they used to play tennis at the same club."

"So, she knew that Chas was here, and after what happened with her sister, it would be easy enough to see why she might try to frame him, but would she have the guts or technical knowledge to cut the judge's brake lines?" Kel wondered.

"Because if she did, she'd be killing two birds with one stone, so to speak," Echo mused. "The judge would be dead, and Chas would go down for the crime. But is she really deluded enough to believe that she'd be smart enough to take down a well-respected detective?"

"Quite possibly. The court documents indicated that she holds a degree in criminal justice. Apparently she chose her major during her sister's trial."

"But wait, something doesn't make sense..." Missy frowned. "Didn't you say that the reason the judge assigned Muffy to community service was because she crashed her car into the side of a bar and grill?"

"That's what the court documents say, yes. Why?" Kel was puzzled.

"What's a wealthy, educated young woman like Muffy Fairchild doing at a bar and grill?" she asked, raising an eyebrow.

"Well, I actually found out a bit about that as well," the artist smiled a secret smile. He had a gift for being able to establish a trusting relationship with strangers, particularly women, in a matter of moments, and that gift had served him well yesterday.

"After researching the court records on Amanda and Muffy and all of that, I figured I'd go have a cocktail and try to puzzle out who might have done what and why," he began.

"You've been reading Summer Prescott books again, haven't you?" Echo asked dryly, making fun of the artist's penchant for cozy mysteries.

"It's a guilty pleasure in which I highly recommend that you indulge," he grinned. "But, at any rate… I saw a gracefully aged woman who looked as though she might have the pulse on the social scene in this part of the world, and I couldn't have been more correct. We talked at length about people, places and parties—we knew some of the same families—and somehow, the subject of Muffy and Amanda came up. As it turns out, Muffy has a preference for, shall we say, walking on the wild side," Kel waggled his eyebrows.

"Do tell," Echo sat forward, resting her chin on her hands.

"There's not much to tell, really. She just apparently delights in finding love on the 'other side of the tracks,'" he shrugged. "She's been seen lately with an ex-race car driver."

"And is connected to a judge who died in a charity exhibition of cars… there has to be a tie-in there somewhere," Missy remarked.

"My thoughts exactly, and I'm having tea with my new friend, the widow Cornwall, to see if she might have any further insight which we'll find useful," Kel nodded.

"You cad, leading on that poor, unsuspecting woman," Echo grinned.

"I'm merely a sacrificial lamb," he chuckled, gazing fondly at his fiancée.

A thought suddenly occurred to Missy. "Hey… has anyone seen Spencer?"

Chapter 12

Chas Beckett was alone in the study of his opulent cottage, deep in thought, pondering who might have a motive to break in to his family's estate, who would have reason to murder Judge Ian Gordon, and if the two crimes might possibly be related. He saw pools of red and blue light flashing by his window, and heard sirens. Missy ran into the study.

"Chas, did you see that? It looks like at least three police cars and an ambulance just drove by. You should see what's happening... maybe you could help," she urged him, kissing his cheek.

"I'll go see what's happening," the detective nodded, wondering what could have possibly happened now, in one of the most security-conscious places on earth.

Climbing into the golf cart, thankful that it had a zip-on wind cover now that the sun had set and the air had a cold bite to it, Chas followed the direction taken by the emergency vehicles. The glow from their still-revolving lights made an easy beacon to follow in the fading twilight. A uniformed officer was blocking the road that led to the cottage where the police cars and ambulance had come to a halt.

The young officer held up a hand to halt the progress of Chas's golf cart.

"I'm sorry, sir, but I can't let you through."

"I'm here to see if I can help," the detective replied, flashing his badge.

"That ID isn't going to even get you close to this scene, Beckett," Detective Wallace Charlton drawled, stepping out of the shadows behind the officer. "In fact, it's awfully interesting that you just happened to show up."

"You've been reading too many crime novels, Charlton. Everyone in the county saw the lights and heard the sirens headed for this scene. With the way that cases get bogged down around here, I thought maybe a seasoned professional should step in," Chas shot back, more than irritated at the smug manner of the detective.

"You can leave the scene now, or be arrested for obstruction of justice and hindering an investigation, Beckett. Your choice," Wallace ground out, red-faced, as the young officer watched the exchange. "But don't even try to leave the resort. You've got some explaining to do."

The detective stalked back toward the cottage, and Chas addressed the uniformed cop.

"So much for a cooperative effort," he joked wryly.

"Sorry about that, sir. Jurisdictional issues," the officer shrugged.

"What happened anyway?" Chas asked, sounding conversational.

"I'm sorry, I'm really not at liberty…" the young man began, stopping when the detective raised his hand.

"I know, I know, I get it. You can't say anything," he nodded with understanding as a new pair of headlights swept onto the road behind him.

Both men were silent as the coroner's car slid slowly past, a somber indicator of what had happened in the luxurious cottage ahead of them.

"Well, that clears up a bit of the mystery," Chas commented to no one in particular.

"Yes, sir," the officer nodded, his eyes following the vehicle.

"Stay warm," the detective raised a hand in farewell and turned the golf cart around, heading back toward his cottage.

When Spencer Bengal had finally, gracefully extricated himself from the company of Muffy Fairchild, he followed the lovely young socialite, instinctively knowing that not all was as it seemed with the young woman. She was staying in a suite at the main lodge, and he waited in a discreet corner of the foyer for her to come down, warding off potential conversations by pretending to read a book.

To her credit, the naturally pretty redhead took scarcely more than an hour and a half to shower and prepare for dinner after her vigorous set of tennis with

Spencer. Surprisingly, instead of heading toward the dining hall, Muffy, dressed casually in designer jeans and a three-thousand dollar plain black sweater, headed for the road that led to the cottages. However, when the young woman reached the tree line, instead of taking the road, she took a furtive look around and slipped into the woods, as if she were making sure that no one watched.

Spencer followed the young woman easily through the woods, slipping through the trees without making a sound, curious as to where she might be going. She crisscrossed through the trails as though on a mission, and the Marine hung back a bit when she approached one of the cottages. As he crouched low behind a stand of vegetation, Spencer watched as a younger man opened a back door to let Muffy in, glancing nervously about. Spencer stayed settled for about an hour until suddenly, just after darkness fell, he saw the young redhead come bursting out the back door, running like her heels were on fire.

"Want me to track her?" Janssen said in a low voice, appearing out of nowhere.

"Yup, do it," Spencer replied, heading down the trail toward Chas and Missy's cottage.

By the time the Marine made it back to the cottage, Chas was just returning home.

"What happened?" Missy asked, wide-eyed with worry, when her husband came in the door.

"I couldn't get past the perimeter that had been established, but I did see the coroner's car go by," the detective sighed.

Spencer came into the kitchen, where Missy was busy making tea, only slightly out of breath after his over two-mile run.

"I think Muffy Fairchild may have just committed murder," he announced calmly.

Chapter 13

Detective Wallace Charlton was no rookie, and he knew a suspicious situation when he saw one. The trembling young man in front of him had nearly encountered a cold-blooded killer, and was having a tough time recovering from it. He'd clearly cared about his employer, who now lay in a puddle of blood in the middle of the kitchen floor.

"I'm sorry to put you through this, Mr. Vance," the detective said to the thin, greasy-haired young man who sat in front of him. "Can you take me through your afternoon again, please?"

"I was tinkering under the hood of Mr. Chapman's car for most of the afternoon. He wanted me to give her a good going-over after the judge's car was tampered with, and then I went for a walk in the woods to just get some fresh air after being underneath the car all day. When I came back… I…" the young man gulped, unable to continue for a moment.

"Where did you enter the residence?" Wallace prompted.

"I came in the front door," Adam Vance answered weakly.

"What happened next?"

"I heard the back door slam, and I thought that it must be the boss coming in, so I walked back to the kitchen," the young man explained, taking shuddering breaths.

"And that's when you found Mr. Chapman on the floor?"

Adam nodded. "The blood, there was so much blood…"

"Then what happened?"

"I saw the knob starting to turn, and I thought that whoever did this might have come back, so I ran to the door and held the knob in place while I locked it.

Then I locked myself in the bathroom and called you guys. I feel like such a coward."

"Don't beat yourself up, you did the right thing. Too many folks have died or been seriously hurt because they tried to be a hero," Detective Charlton assured the pale young man who stared at the floor, his knees shaking.

"What's the nature of your relationship with Mr. Chapman?"

"He's my boss. I take care of his cars and drive for him in races and exhibitions, things like that."

"How long have you been working for him?"

"Just a few months. I was a semi-pro race car driver, but I lost my sponsor, so I had to find something else."

"Do you know of anyone who might have a grudge against Mr. Chapman? Or who might want him dead?"

Adam Vance shook his head and touched his shadow of a mustache with one hand. "No idea. It's pretty weird though, that the owners of two of the last three of those cars ended up dead," he shrugged, looking uncomfortable.

"Was Mr. Chapman acquainted with Judge Gordon, to your knowledge?"

"No, not that I know of," Adam shook his head.

"What about the third owner? Was Mr. Chapman acquainted with Charles Beckett?"

"Not really. I think he might have tried to buy the identical car from him, but I'm not sure."

"I see," Wallace nodded, closing his notebook. "Thank you for your time, Mr. Vance, that's all for now. Will you be on the resort for a while, in case I have more questions?"

"I... uh... I don't think I can... you know... sleep here after this. So, I'll probably go to a hotel or something," the young man swallowed hard, clearly upset.

"Not a problem," Charlton held a business card out to him. "Give me a call once you get settled in somewhere. If I don't answer, just leave a message as to where you are."

"Yes, sir," Adam nodded, standing up and moving, as though in a daze, to the door.

Wallace Charlton turned to a uniformed officer standing nearby. "Williams, go to cottage 1968 and pick up Chas Beckett. Don't arrest him, just bring him in for questioning, and if he gives you any hassle, call me," he ordered grimly.

Chapter 14

The world seemed to be moving in a most unpleasant manner when Muffy Fairchild woke up, shivering, nauseated, and unable to see because of a heavy cloth that was tied over her eyes. She tried to sit up, but was restrained by an unseen hand.

"Not so fast, darlin'," a low, gravelly voice drawled. "There's nowhere to go and no way to get there, so you might as well relax and answer my questions."

"Who are you? What's going on?" the redhead demanded, frightened but reverting back to her typically imperious nature.

"I guess you didn't hear me the first time, but it's gonna be me askin' the questions, not you, sweetheart, so you might as well quit squirmin' and cooperate," Janssen advised, patiently prepared to keep her in the rowboat in the middle of the lake all night if he had to.

"Why does the ground keep moving? Who are you?" the socialite began to panic, realizing that her hands and feet were bound.

"You ain't exactly a fast learner, are ya?" the veteran sighed, thinking that it was going to be a long night.

"Are you going to kill me?" Muffy asked quietly.

"Well now, that's an ironic question, considering your recent activities, ain't it?"

"I don't know what you're talking about," she retorted weakly.

"Oh, you don't? Well, let's see if I can break it down for you. You come running out of one of them lake houses, clothes all bloody, weapon in your hand dripping with blood, and pretty soon there's lights and sirens all over the place. Ringin' any bells, princess?" Janssen drawled, flicking a used toothpick into the frigid lake water.

Muffy Fairchild was not the sharpest knife in the drawer, but she knew when she'd been busted, and remained silent.

"You know how to swim, darlin'?"

"Oh please, I was winning swim meets when I was five," she replied snottily.

"That's good, cuz if you don't start talkin', I'm gonna toss you out in the middle of this lake and it's a heckuva long way back to shore," the Marine mused, cleaning his fingernails with a long hunting blade.

"I have nothing to say to you, whoever you are," the redhead declared haughtily.

"Really? That's a shame. I'd hate to have to persuade you," he said, re-sheathing his knife so it made a distinctive metallic rasp.

"What do you want from me?" Muffy whispered, after hearing the sound.

"You can start by tellin' me who you killed and why."

"I didn't kill anyone," she insisted, her voice trembling.

"Then why were you running through the woods with a bloody knife, covered in blood?" Janssen asked, his voice skeptical.

Muffy sighed. "It's a long story."

"I've got all night, princess."

Chapter 15

"This kind of behavior is going to cause an indelible mark on your service record, Charlton," Chas observed mildly, after being transported to the police station in the back of a patrol car.

"Don't threaten me, Beckett," the detective sneered from across the interrogation table. "For once, you're not in charge. You're the bad guy here, not the knight in shining armor that you've managed to convince everyone in this county that you are. I don't care who your daddy was, or what cases you may have solved in the past, you're going down in flames this time, *buddy*, and I'm going to sit back and roast marshmallows," Wallace violated Chas's personal space, his face an inch from the impassive detective, chin jutted forward in an ugly grimace.

"It's unfortunate that with every ridiculous sentence that you utter, you're showing yourself to be a gutless and petty man, rather than doing your job and acting like a detective," Beckett replied with a rueful sigh.

"Gutless and petty, huh? You must be looking in the mirror when you say that, because, by the way, it wasn't me who murdered a judge and a prominent business man for his own gain," Wallace taunted.

"Really? I have no way of knowing whether or not that's true, actually," Chas raised an eyebrow. "Okay, Charlton, enough of this. Time's a-wasting, and there's a murderer on the loose out there somewhere, so let's get to the bottom of this, shall we?"

"Yeah, let's get to the bottom of it," Wallace snarled, sitting back, much to Chas's relief. He couldn't help but notice that the man was in dire need of a breath mint.

"Judge Gordon offered to buy your daddy's car collection, and Mr. Chapman offered to buy just your Champagne Elite car, isn't that correct?"

"Yes."

"And you told both of them no, didn't you?"

"Yes."

"And then you killed them both because your car would be worth more if the other two didn't exist, isn't that correct?"

"That's preposterous," Chas fought hard to resist the urge to roll his eyes. "As you've seen fit to remind me again and again, I have no need to increase my assets. I have more money than I can possibly use in a lifetime. Why would I go to such lengths to raise the value of one of my cars? It's a museum piece already, there's no need to increase its value."

Just then, the door to the interrogation room burst open. Wallace turned, angry at the interruption until he saw who had blazed into the room.

"Charlton," the chief of police thundered. "What's the meaning of this? When I told you to lay off of Chas Beckett, I meant it."

Wallace Charlton ran a finger under the collar of his shirt, his bluster and cocksure certainty gone.

"I... there's been a turn of events... and I..." he began.

"I've read the report, and you've inconvenienced Detective Beckett for long enough. Get out," he ordered.

When Charlton had huffed from the room, the chief took a seat across from Chas.

"Wallace is a buffoon," he rasped, without preamble.

"So it would seem," Chas raised an eyebrow.

"What do you think is going on here, Beckett? I could use your expertise on this one."

"Well, the only tie-in that we know of between the two victims, is the Champagne Elite car. I would think that the question that we should be asking is... who would have a deadly interest in the cars?" the detective shrugged.

The chief opened his mouth to answer and shut it again when a uniformed officer poked his head into the interrogation room.

"I'm sorry to interrupt, Chief, Detective," he nodded to acknowledge the men. "But there's someone in the lobby that you both need to see." The cop exited the room with the chief and Chas at his heels.

When they came around the corner, they were astounded to see Spencer, leading a young woman covered in blood and holding a large knife toward another interrogation room. Chas and Spencer exchanged a glance, and the detective gave the Marine a slight nod.

Chapter 16

A malignant presence lurked outside the window of cottage #1968, as the occupant inside fretted about what was happening to her beloved husband.

Missy was worried to death. Chas had been taken to the police station in connection with the murder of yet another resort guest, and she hadn't heard from him in hours. Echo and Kel had gone back to their cottage for the evening and she didn't want to disturb them, and Spencer was nowhere to be found, so Missy paced back and forth in front of the television, telling herself to sit down to watch a movie but entirely unable to comply.

She missed Toffee and Bitsy, her golden retriever and maltipoo, who were at home in Florida, under the watchful eye of Maggie the innkeeper. Missy just wanted to go back to her normal life, baking cupcakes and meeting guests from all over the country and the world at breakfast each morning. Life as the wife of a super-wealthy detective wasn't especially difficult when one wasn't constantly surrounded by reminders of the differences in their backgrounds. Chas's life in New York had been an entirely different experience from anything to which she'd ever been exposed, and she was clearly an outsider.

Needing something to calm her jittery nerves, Missy went to the kitchen to pour herself a glass of wine. The marble tile floor was cold on her bare feet as she stretched to reach a fine crystal glass, which she set on the granite countertop while she looked for a corkscrew in one of the many kitchen drawers. Finally finding the elusive tool, she selected a full-bodied red, and poured it, wondering whether or not she should take her wine out to the hot tub for optimal relaxation while she waited for Chas to come home.

She heard the knob on the back porch door rattle, and looked up expectantly, thinking that it would certainly be Chas; however, when she saw a man in a black mask burst into the kitchen, her wineglass shattered on the floor. Missy fled the room, wincing as she stepped on broken crystal on her way. She ran as fast as she could toward the guest bedroom, hoping to hide in the closet before the intruder navigated his way around the kitchen island and down the hall to catch up with her. She heard footsteps pounding through the kitchen after her, but she made it through the bedroom and into the closet without the frightening stranger catching up with her.

Her heart beat so loudly that she feared he'd hear it from the hallway, so she tried to slow her breathing, making as little sound as possible from behind Chas's suits and her dresses. There was silence for a very long time, then she heard someone moving around in the guest bedroom, the footsteps seeming to head directly for the closet where she was hiding. The sound that came next—a dark, sinister chuckle—made her blood run cold.

Muffy Fairchild sat across the interrogation table from the chief of police and Chas Beckett, whom she'd idolized from the time that she could walk. Her clothing was stiff with Irving Chapman's blood and her hands bore cuts from the knife with which he'd been killed. The socialite had certainly had better days.

The chief asked her questions, but her answers were always directed toward Chas, the young man who had briefly dated her sister and stolen her heart at an impressionable age.

"Did you kill Irving Chapman?" the chief asked somberly.

"No, I didn't. I really didn't. You have to believe me, Charles… " she began, stopping when the detective held up his hand.

"Let's allow the chief to ask his questions, okay?" he said calmly, hoping to get Muffy to focus.

"Okay," she nodded, twisting her bloodstained hands in her lap, the murder weapon laying on the table in front of the chief.

"Who killed Irving Chapman, Miss Fairchild?"

She hesitated for a fraction of a second, and Chas leaned forward, not wanting to lose momentum.

"Muff, who did this? Who put you in this situation?" he asked in his kindest older brother voice.

His kindness was her undoing. "Adam Vance," she blurted, bursting into tears which combined with the streaks of blood, sending crimson rivulets down her cheeks.

Spencer, who was standing silently in the corner with his arms crossed, looked at Chas, who then looked at the chief, while Muffy sobbed hot red tears into the sleeve of her expensive sweater. Clearly, the name didn't ring a bell with any of them.

"Muffy, look at me," Chas urged, trying to get more information out of her. When she complied, sniffling, her breath hitching, he began again.

"Who is Adam Vance?"

"He worked for Mr. Chapman. He took care of his cars and drove for him in races and exhibitions," she explained, taking the tissue that Chas handed her, and gazing at it in horror when she saw the streaks of blood.

Noticing her sudden pallor, Spencer went out into the hall and came back with a cup of ice water, and put it in front of the shivering socialite.

"Why would he kill his boss? That doesn't make sense," the chief interjected as Muffy took small sips from the paper cup, looking a bit stronger.

"Because Chapman knew…" her voice trailed off and she stared miserably at the tabletop.

"Knew what?" Chas and the chief asked in unison as Spencer's eyes bored into the back of the young woman's head.

"That Adam had… had…" Muffy burst into tears again, and Chas had to pause and take a breath, despite his frustration.

When she'd had a few moments for tears, he tried again.

"What did Chapman know?"

"That Adam had… killed Judge Gordon. But it was an accident. He didn't mean to, he really didn't—he's actually very sweet. Chapman had told him to cut the brake line on the judge's car so that he'd drop out of the race, and there'd be minimal damage to the car, but when Adam cut the lines, the judge drove it anyway and then there was the crash and…" she trailed off again, sniveling.

"Why would Chapman want the judge dead?" the chief wondered aloud.

Muffy shook her head. "He didn't want him dead, he just wanted his car. The death was an accident."

"Does the "accident" have anything to do with why you tried to break into my family's estate after the race?" Chas asked quietly.

The young socialite was startled and stared at the chief wide-eyed.

"How...?" she stammered.

"It wasn't terribly difficult to figure out. We caught a glimpse of someone with your build on the security cameras, and I'm betting that those jogging shoes that you're wearing match the footprint left outside the wall. Why were you trying to break in?"

"Because Adam had told me that I needed to plant the pair of bolt cutters that he'd used on the judge's car somewhere that would make it look like you had done it," the redhead admitted miserably.

"And when you got startled at the estate..." he led her.

"I left them on the porch at your cottage," Muffy finished with a sob.

"I still don't understand… why did Chapman want the car so badly?" Chas asked, baffled.

"Because he'd lost almost all of his money in failed speculation. The car that he had would've financed him for years if he could eliminate all of the others. He planned to buy the judge's then try to find some way to get you to part with yours. He was going to destroy them both, making his valuable enough to give him some leverage in buying back into the market. He didn't care about the cars, it was about the money for him," Muffy's head dropped to her chest.

"That explains why Chapman accidentally killed Judge Gordon by having Adam cut the brake lines, but it doesn't even come close to explaining why Adam killed Chapman," Chas stared her down. "What could possibly have made him murder his employer? That's rather self-defeating, don't you think?" he challenged.

"Adam killed Chapman because Chapman said that he wanted to go to the police and tell them the truth about the judge's murder. He planned to blame the entire thing on Adam, and they would've believed him, because of the influence that he still had. Adam refused to go back to prison, so I guess he just decided to take care of things his own way," her shoulders bowed inward, as though she bore the weight of the world on them.

"And why, exactly, if Adam killed his boss, were you the one fleeing the scene with the murder weapon?" the chief asked skeptically.

"He told me to get rid of it. He said he'd sell the car and that we could go to the Caribbean and live our lives on the beach," she said wistfully.

"So you were in an intimate relationship with Mr. Vance," the chief drilled her with a glance.

"I… uh, yes… we… dated," she said lamely, the color rising in her cheeks.

"But, if his goal was to sell the car for the highest price, what was he planning to do about my car?" Chas asked, a horrible realization dawning.

"I…" Muffy's eyes filled with tears, her mouth agape.

"Missy," Spencer said grimly, bolting from the room.

Chapter 17

Missy began to feel faint and guessed that it may have had something to do with trying so hard to control her breathing.

"Come out, come out, wherever you are," a thin male voice taunted from outside the door. "Thought you were clever, didn't you? You might have been able to successfully hide in the closet, if it hadn't been for that pesky trail of blood that you left. Look down, doll. Your very lifeblood is seeping out under the door. You might say it's a 'dead' giveaway," he emitted that awful chuckle again.

"I'm going to count to three," he began, as Missy swayed within the closet, faint from blood loss. The cut on her foot had been deeper than she'd realized, and it had betrayed her.

"And once I'm done, I'm going to come in and cut you up into little tiny... OOF!" the madman's threat was cut off and Missy heard the sound of two bodies hitting the floor before she slumped there herself, unable to hang in there any longer.

Spencer and Chas burst through the cottage door, stepping over a discarded wetsuit on the front porch with barely a passing glance. They ran through the living room, saw the trail of blood that led to the guest room, and stumbled quite literally over the prone form of Adam Vance at the foot of the bed, unconscious and neatly bound with duct tape. Chas spotted the pool of blood seeping under the closet door and opened it to find Missy slumped inside.

Dashing to her side, he took her in his arms and she stirred, causing him to exhale with relief. Spencer had knelt beside the couple, his trained eyes assessing her overall condition. Glancing over at the still-inert form of Adam Vance, his jaw tightened and he started to rise, but Chas's hand on his arm stopped him. The detective said nothing, just gave a brief shake of his head.

"I'm guessing that whoever did the handiwork with the duct tape might not want to be discovered," Chas said meaningfully, eyeing the madman.

Spencer nodded, then quickly moved to Vance and removed the duct tape, taking it to the trash in the garage. By the time he came back into the guest room, the police and an ambulance had arrived and were dealing with Missy and Adam.

Chapter 18

The black stretch limo carrying Echo, Kel, Spencer, Chas, and a bandaged and subdued Missy pulled up to the front gates of the Beckett estate. After a brief stop so that Chas could meet with Chalmers, the friends were headed to the airport for their flight back to Florida. As the limo glided up the private drive, Spencer fixed his attention on a transaction that was taking place on the front steps of the mansion, between Chalmers and a scarred, long-haired young man with a military backpack, who looked like a vagrant.

The servant handed the young man a bundle, and after receiving it, he locked eyes for a brief moment with

Spencer, who had the window of the limo rolled halfway down, then disappeared into the forest.

"Friend of yours?" Kel nudged the Marine with a grin.

Spencer shook his head, saying nothing as Missy gazed at him, her brow furrowed.

They piled out of the limo, taking advantage of their last few minutes on the estate, and Chas approached Chalmers.

"Helping the homeless?" he asked the servant with a concerned frown.

"No, Master Charles, at least not in that particular case," he nodded toward the woods where the young man had disappeared. "The lad took care of some things around here for me. I was merely paying him what I owed him. He might not look like it, but he's quite a reliable chap, sir," Chalmers assured him.

"Well, I certainly trust your judgment in these things," Chas smiled at the creased and crinkled man who had been a constant in his life.

"Your father would have approved, sir," he replied enigmatically, glancing briefly at Spencer.

"Master Bengal, may I speak with you for a moment?" he asked.

Spencer moved wordlessly to his side and followed the elderly servant into his office, returning a few minutes later.

"What was that all about?" Missy blinked at the Marine, feeling as though she was watching the surface of a pond ripple, while underneath a battle of sea creatures raged, unseen.

"Oh, he just wanted to thank me for my service," Spencer smiled politely, then looked away, as Chas gazed at him speculatively.

"How is it that he knew you'd served?" Kel wondered aloud.

"His military bearing, obviously," Chas dismissed the question. "Look at that posture… it's evident that that came from training. Everyone ready to go?" he changed the subject, putting his arm around Missy's waist as she leaned on her crutch.

"More than," she sighed, leaning into him.

Chas took her crutch from her, handing it to Spencer, and swung his bride up into his arms, gingerly carrying her to the limo and setting her inside.

Chapter 19

"Is it weird that I'm much more relaxed here in Florida than I was when on vacation?" Echo asked, sipping her coffee as she, Kel, and Missy gathered around their favorite bistro table in Cupcakes in Paradise.

"It's not weird at all," Missy shook her head. "I feel the same way. Even though I have day-to-day responsibilities, I'm so glad to be home. I wish I fit in better with Chas's family, though," she mused ruefully.

"I don't think he would have married you if you did," her friend snickered.

"There certainly is something to be said for being a mere peasant," Kel chuckled. "It's much easier on the soul, I think."

Echo nodded, taking a bite of her cupcake, and Missy giggled.

"Well, this particular peasant had plenty of time to rethink the path that her life is taking…" she began.

"And?" Echo prompted, setting down her coffee cup.

"And… I'm not going to close the cupcake shop. I love what I do, and if I start feeling overwhelmed again, I'll hire some help," she said firmly, her mind made up.

"That's great! I'm so happy for you," Echo grinned. "But I can't help but feel like I'm to blame for making you feel overwhelmed," she sobered.

Kel frowned. "I know you dear ladies are attached at the hip, but how on earth could Missy's stress be your fault?" he asked, incredulous.

"I'd like to know that too," Missy leaned forward, puzzled.

"I used to help out here every day, and then, when I started working as Kel's gallery manager, I only worked mornings. Now that I have my candle shop, I only come in for coffee. I feel like if I had been more loyal, you wouldn't be so stressed out," she confessed, her eyes pleading for understanding.

"You silly goose," Missy reached over and hugged her best friend. "Not only were you here when I needed you most, you even moved here from California because I wouldn't stop hounding you. You've helped me build everything that I've built here, and I couldn't be happier that you've finally found your own groove. Your candle shop is amazing, and I'm so happy that you're successful and happy—I wouldn't have it any other way," she reassured her.

"You sure?" Echo asked.

"Positive," Missy nodded happily. "I'll even let you help me choose a new employee when I need one."

"Can he be as hot as Spencer?" Echo teased, with a sidelong glance at her fiancé.

"Umm… I was thinking a nice, grandmotherly woman, actually," her friend chuckled.

"I second that," Kel piped up, looking at his bride-to-be with mock admonition.

"I think I'll need the help sooner rather than later," Missy said seriously.

"Oh, why?" Echo asked.

"Because my dear, you and I have to go to Louisiana to plan Grayson's wedding, and we have to start looking at plans for yours as well."

Missy had given the cupcake shop that she'd run in LaChance, Louisiana to Grayson, who had been one of her trusted managers and had become like a son to her. He'd asked her to plan his wedding and she'd joyfully agreed.

"Right, forgot about that," Echo joked as Kel sputtered indignantly.

Chapter 20

Spencer's mind was far away as he headed toward a remote spot that had become a bit of a refuge for him. He didn't have to think about where he was going, he just drove on instinct, his thoughts elsewhere. He drove down the overgrown dirt path as far as he was able, then parked the car and started jogging toward the cabin that had become a symbol of sanity and hope in a sometimes less than sane and hopeful world.

He carried with him a six-pack of ice-cold craft beer in a small nylon cooler, and his stride was so smooth as he ran that it didn't jostle the bottles at all. He reached the clearing in front of the small building in short order, despite having taken the time to watch carefully for snakes, gators, and other dangerous wildlife along his route, and climbed the porch steps.

As a matter of habit, he eased himself onto the bare wood of the porch, his back against the rough-hewn siding. He closed his eyes and knew before he opened them again that he wasn't alone.

"You got a funny definition of a vacation, man," Janssen remarked, twisting open a beer.

"You more than earned these," Spencer took a bottle out of the cooler and pushed the nylon tote toward his fellow veteran, who made no secret of the fact that he enjoyed a fine IPA every now and again.

"It's a shame that hot little redhead had to go to jail," the scarred young man remarked, taking a slug of his beer.

"She won't have it nearly as bad as the loser who actually killed the guys," Spencer replied, his jaw tightening as he remembered Missy's condition when he and Chas had found her in the closet. "You left your wetsuit behind, by the way," he smirked.

"Nah," Janssen drawled. "Wasn't my wetsuit."

"You stole it?"

"Heck, no. I may be many things, but a thief ain't one of 'em," the veteran protested mildly. "That's why I left it behind. Not my fault if the owner was careless enough to leave their boathouse locked with a lock so pitiful that they might as well not've bothered."

Spencer grinned and shook his head, thinking what a relief it was to be able to be in the company of someone who knew exactly who and what he was and accepted him anyway.

"I even left some instructions for the nice security folk at the Pinnacle as to how they might want to improve their perimeter security," Janssen rasped, amused.

"How very kind of you."

"Yeah, I'm just a heckuva guy," he nodded, polishing off his first beer and reaching for another.

"You gonna be around for a while?" Spencer asked, not looking at his buddy.

The scarred veteran shrugged. "Never know. Depends on which way the wind blows. We both took a risk, being up there. We won't know for a while yet whether anyone saw us. I'll keep my ear to the ground and do what I gotta do, you know?"

The Marine nodded. "I hear ya."

"We got a job to do."

"I know."

"If things go south, you're gonna have to make some hard choices, man," Janssen warned.

Spencer's jaw was set. "I've made my choices. I have a family now, that's all there is to it," he insisted softly.

"You and I both know it ain't that easy," was the pragmatic reply. "But I got your back, man. You can bet on that." Janssen stared out into the distance.

"I do. That means a lot," Spencer replied, his gaze faraway.

"It's what we do."

"It's what we do," the Marine agreed.

The two of them sat in silence, Janssen drinking the rest of the six-pack, Spencer lost in the contentment of being in the company of someone who really understood. The sun began to set and Janssen slipped off to his nighttime dwelling, leaving the Marine to think his thoughts and eventually head back to home and family, carrying his empty six-pack.

Author's Note

I'd love to hear your thoughts on my books, the storylines, and anything else that you'd like to comment on—reader feedback is very important to me. My contact information, along with some other helpful links, is listed on the next page. If you'd like to be on my list of "folks to contact" with updates, release and sales notifications, etc.... just shoot me an email and let me know. Thanks for reading!

Also…

… if you're looking for more great reads, Summer Prescott Books publishes several popular series by outstanding Cozy Mystery authors.

Manufactured by Amazon.ca
Bolton, ON